STAR WARS®

THE CLONE WARS™

IN SERVICE OF THE REPUBLIC
VOLUME TWO

A FROZEN DOOM!

SCRIPT
**HENRY GILROY
STEVEN MELCHING**

PENCILS
SCOTT HEPBURN

INKS
DAN PARSONS

COLORS
MICHAEL E. WIGGAM

LETTERING
MICHAEL HEISLER

COVER ART
SCOTT HEPBURN WITH
BRAD ANDERSON

The battle rages for a vital fuel supply! The planet Khorm has been occupied by a droid army that has enslaved the native inhabitants and now hoards their valuable resources. Jedi generals Plo Koon and Kit Fisto lead their clones to liberate the icy world from the traitorous warlord Unger Gout.

With their ships grounded by an artificially created atmospheric storm, the Jedi's initial ground attack is victorious, in spite of tactical blunders by an ambitious officer, Captain Kendal Ozzel.

Now the Jedi lead a mission to destroy the weather-control station, unaware that their earlier victory has been overthrown and that, captured and interrogated by Asajj Ventress, Ozzel has revealed the Jedi's plans . . .

DARK HORSE COMICS

Visit us at www.abdopublishing.com

Reinforced library bound edition published in 2011 by Spotlight, a division of the ABDO Group, 8000 West 78th Street, Edina, Minnesota 55439. Spotlight produces high-quality reinforced library bound editions for schools and libraries. Published by agreement with Dark Horse Comics, Inc., and Lucasfilm Ltd.

Printed in the United States of America, North Mankato, Minnesota.
102010
012011
♻This book contains at least 10% recycled materials..

Cataloging-in-Publication Data

Gilroy, Henry.
  In service of the Republic Vol. 2: a frozen doom! / story, Henry Gilroy and Steve Melching ; art, Scott Hepburn. --Reinforced library bound ed.
      v. cm. -- (Star wars: the clone wars)
      "Dark Horse Comics."
  ISBN 978-1-59961-839-5 (v. 2)
  1. Graphic novels. [1. Graphic novels.] I. Melching, Steve. II. Hepburn, Scott, ill. III. Star Wars, the clone wars (television program) IV. Title.
  PZ7.7.G55Se 2011
  741.5'973

All Spotlight books have reinforced library bindings and are manufactured in the United States of America.

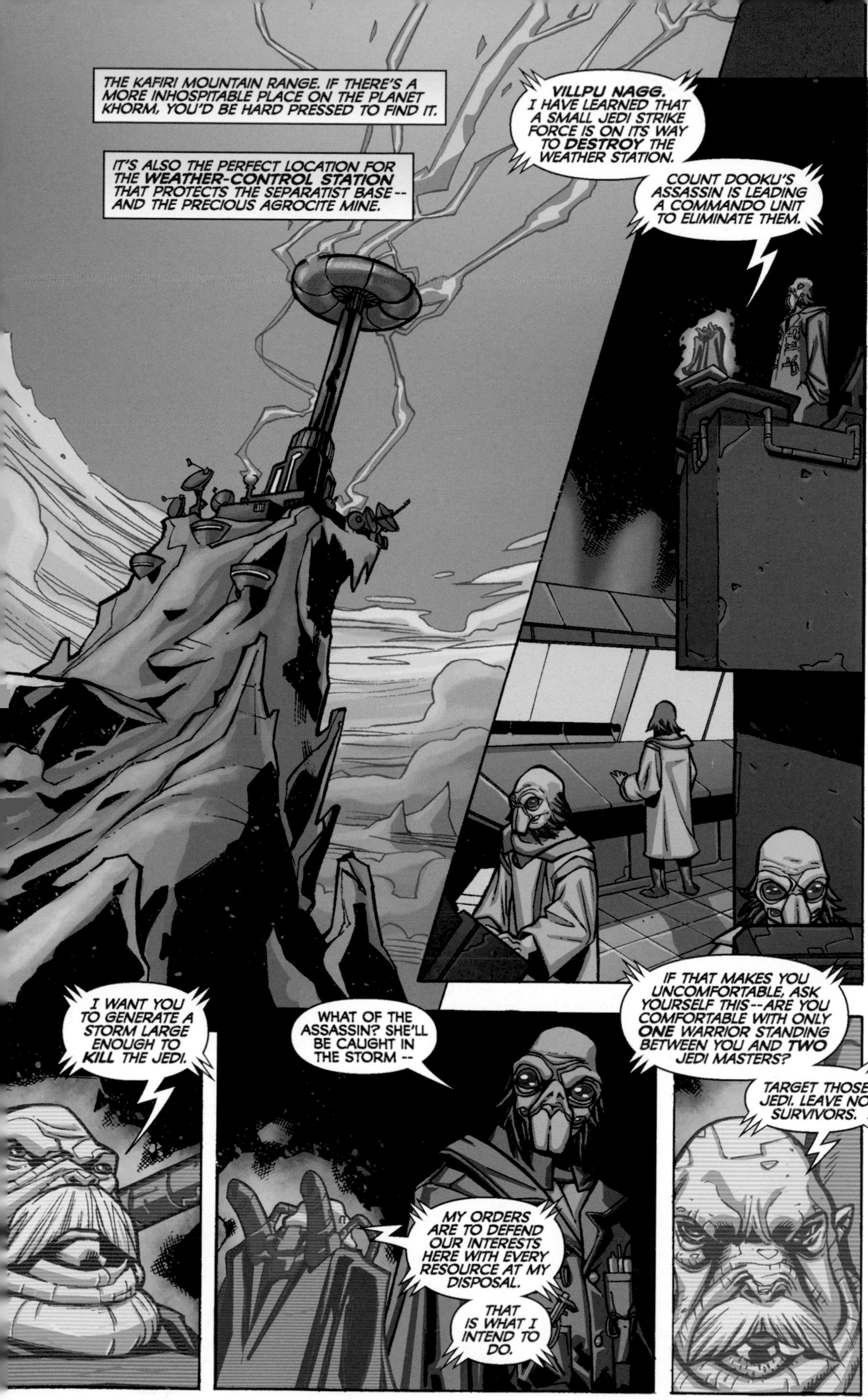
THE KAFIRI MOUNTAIN RANGE. IF THERE'S A MORE INHOSPITABLE PLACE ON THE PLANET KHORM, YOU'D BE HARD PRESSED TO FIND IT.
IT'S ALSO THE PERFECT LOCATION FOR THE WEATHER-CONTROL STATION THAT PROTECTS THE SEPARATIST BASE -- AND THE PRECIOUS AGROCITE MINE.
VILLPU NAGG. I HAVE LEARNED THAT A SMALL JEDI STRIKE FORCE IS ON ITS WAY TO DESTROY THE WEATHER STATION.
COUNT DOOKU'S ASSASSIN IS LEADING A COMMANDO UNIT TO ELIMINATE THEM.
I WANT YOU TO GENERATE A STORM LARGE ENOUGH TO KILL THE JEDI.
WHAT OF THE ASSASSIN? SHE'LL BE CAUGHT IN THE STORM --
MY ORDERS ARE TO DEFEND OUR INTERESTS HERE WITH EVERY RESOURCE AT MY DISPOSAL.
THAT IS WHAT I INTEND TO DO.
IF THAT MAKES YOU UNCOMFORTABLE, ASK YOURSELF THIS--ARE YOU COMFORTABLE WITH ONLY ONE WARRIOR STANDING BETWEEN YOU AND TWO JEDI MASTERS?
TARGET THOSE JEDI. LEAVE NO SURVIVORS.

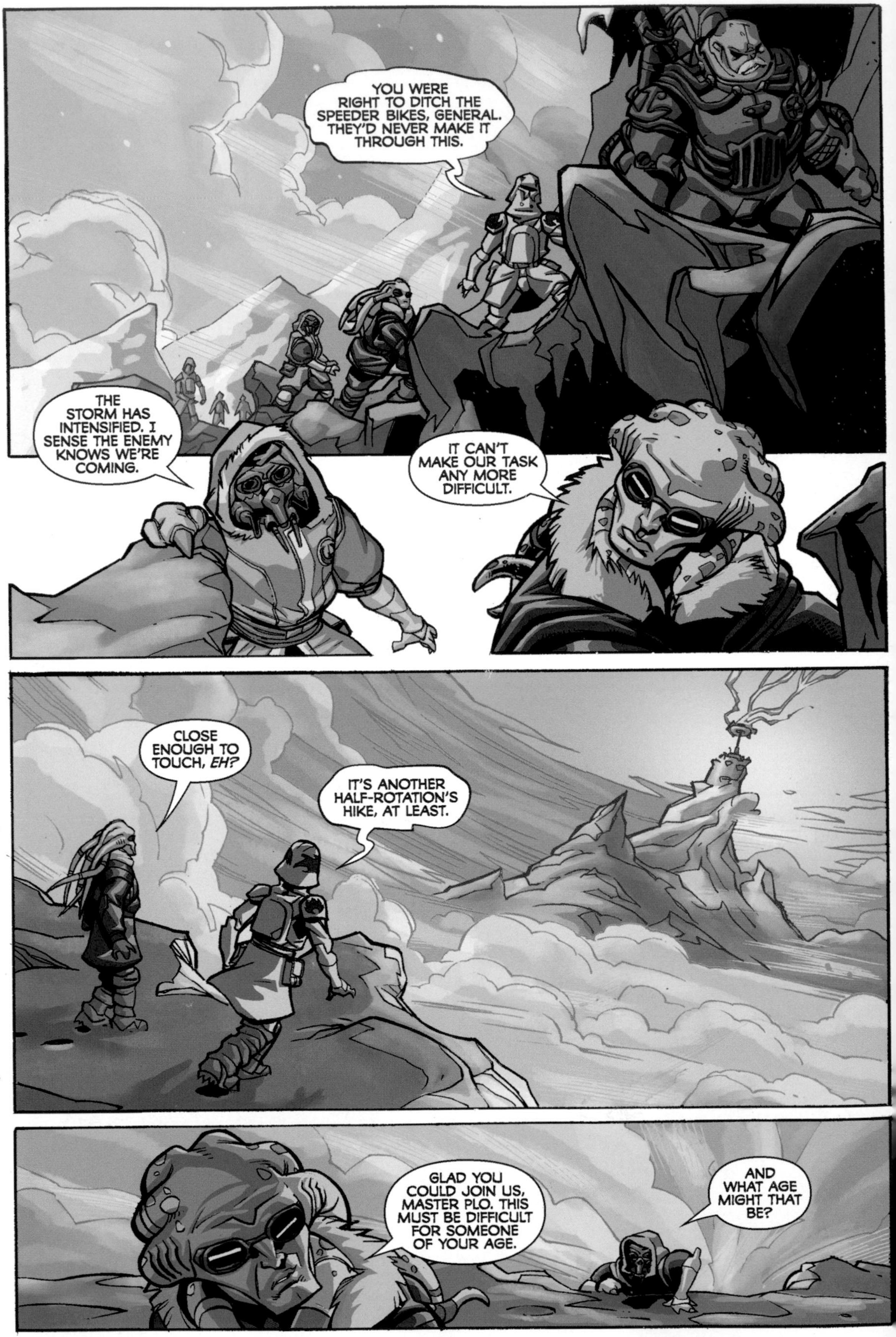
YOU WERE RIGHT TO DITCH THE SPEEDER BIKES, GENERAL. THEY'D NEVER MAKE IT THROUGH THIS.
THE STORM HAS INTENSIFIED. I SENSE THE ENEMY KNOWS WE'RE COMING.
IT CAN'T MAKE OUR TASK ANY MORE DIFFICULT.
CLOSE ENOUGH TO TOUCH, *EH?*
IT'S ANOTHER HALF-ROTATION'S HIKE, AT LEAST.
GLAD YOU COULD JOIN US, MASTER PLO. THIS MUST BE DIFFICULT FOR SOMEONE OF YOUR AGE.
AND WHAT AGE MIGHT THAT BE?

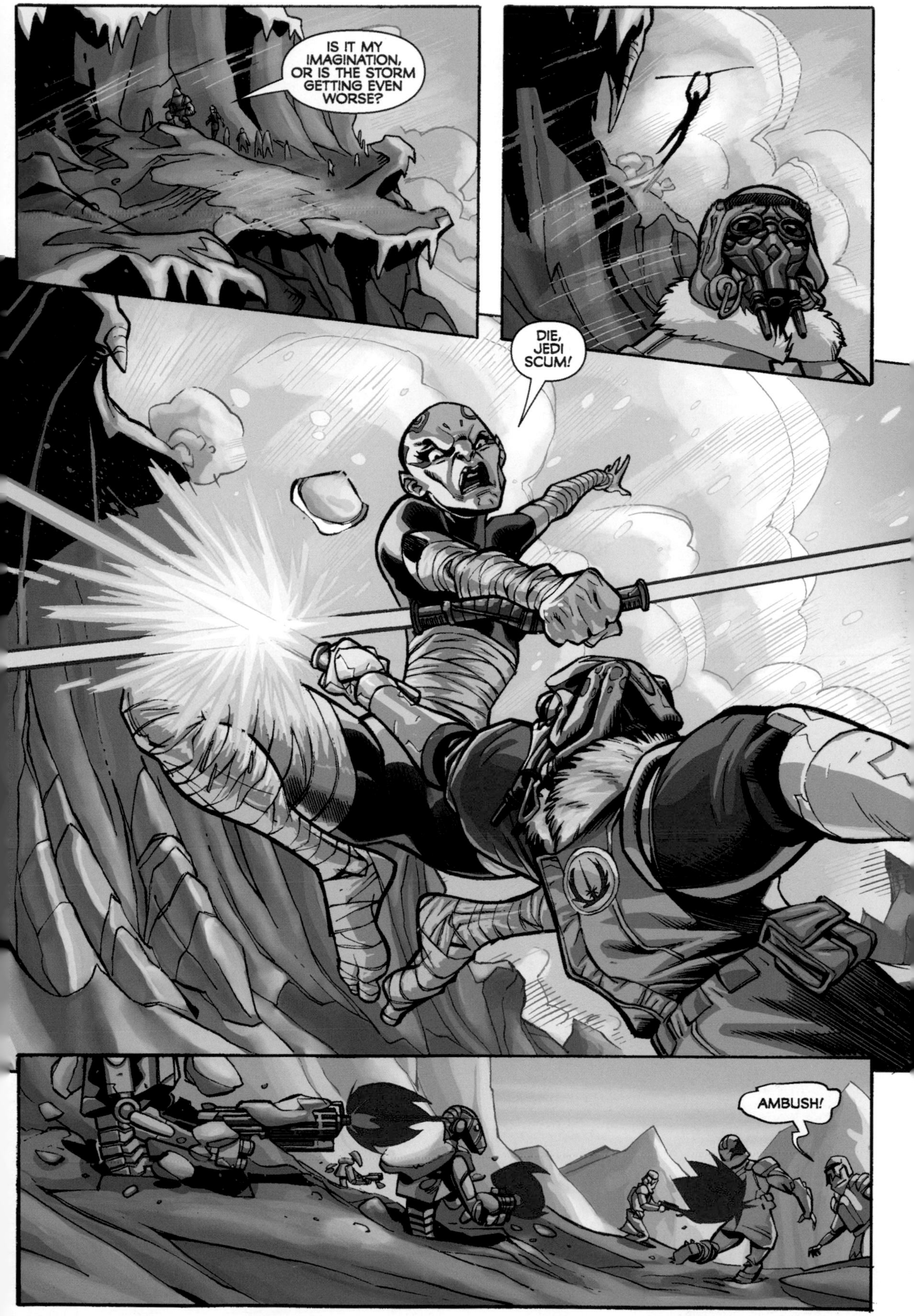
IS IT MY IMAGINATION, OR IS THE STORM GETTING EVEN WORSE?
DIE, JEDI SCUM!
AMBUSH!

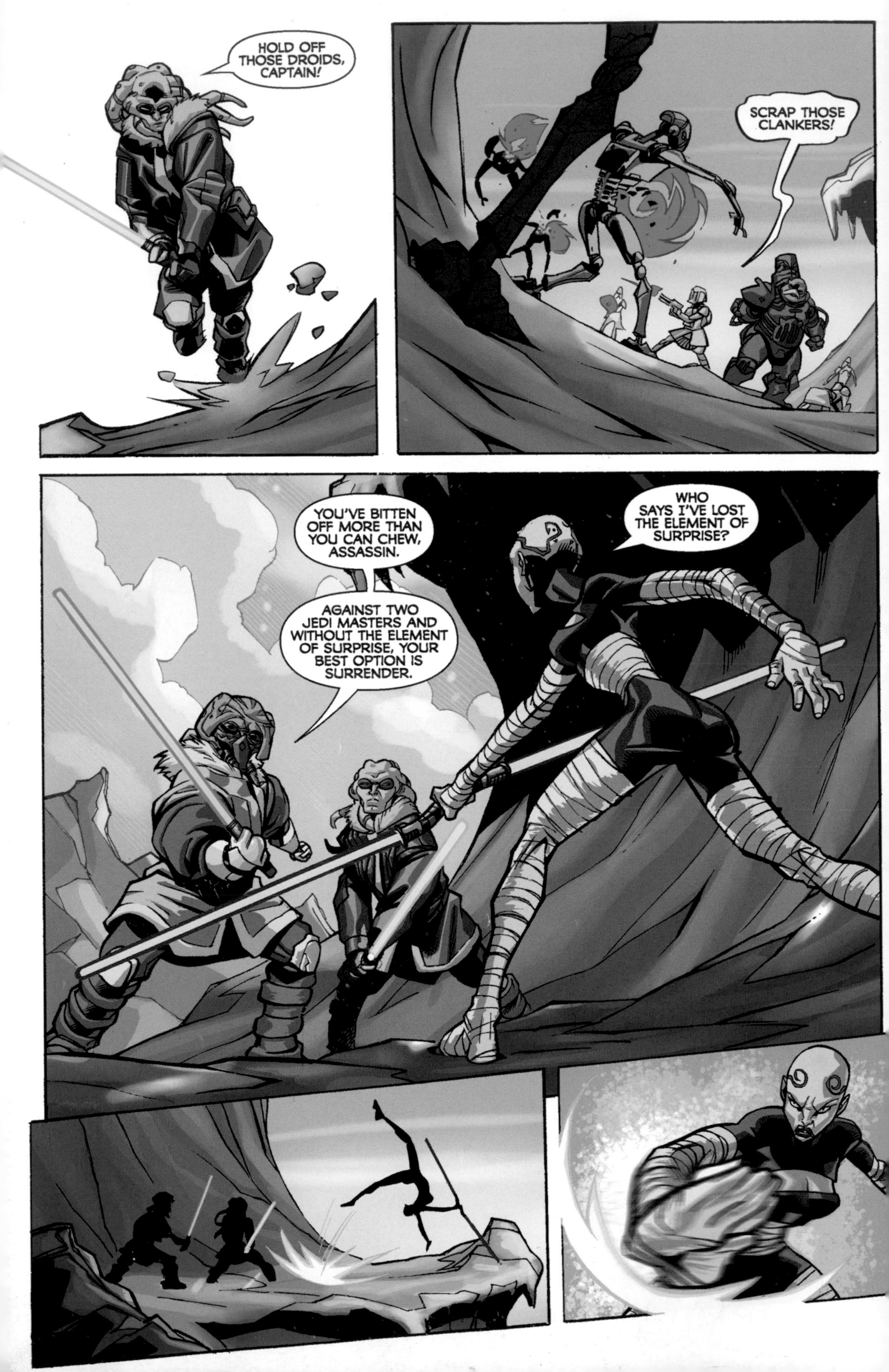
HOLD OFF THOSE DROIDS, CAPTAIN!
SCRAP THOSE CLANKERS!
YOU'VE BITTEN OFF MORE THAN YOU CAN CHEW, ASSASSIN.
AGAINST TWO JEDI MASTERS AND WITHOUT THE ELEMENT OF SURPRISE, YOUR BEST OPTION IS SURRENDER.
WHO SAYS I'VE LOST THE ELEMENT OF SURPRISE?

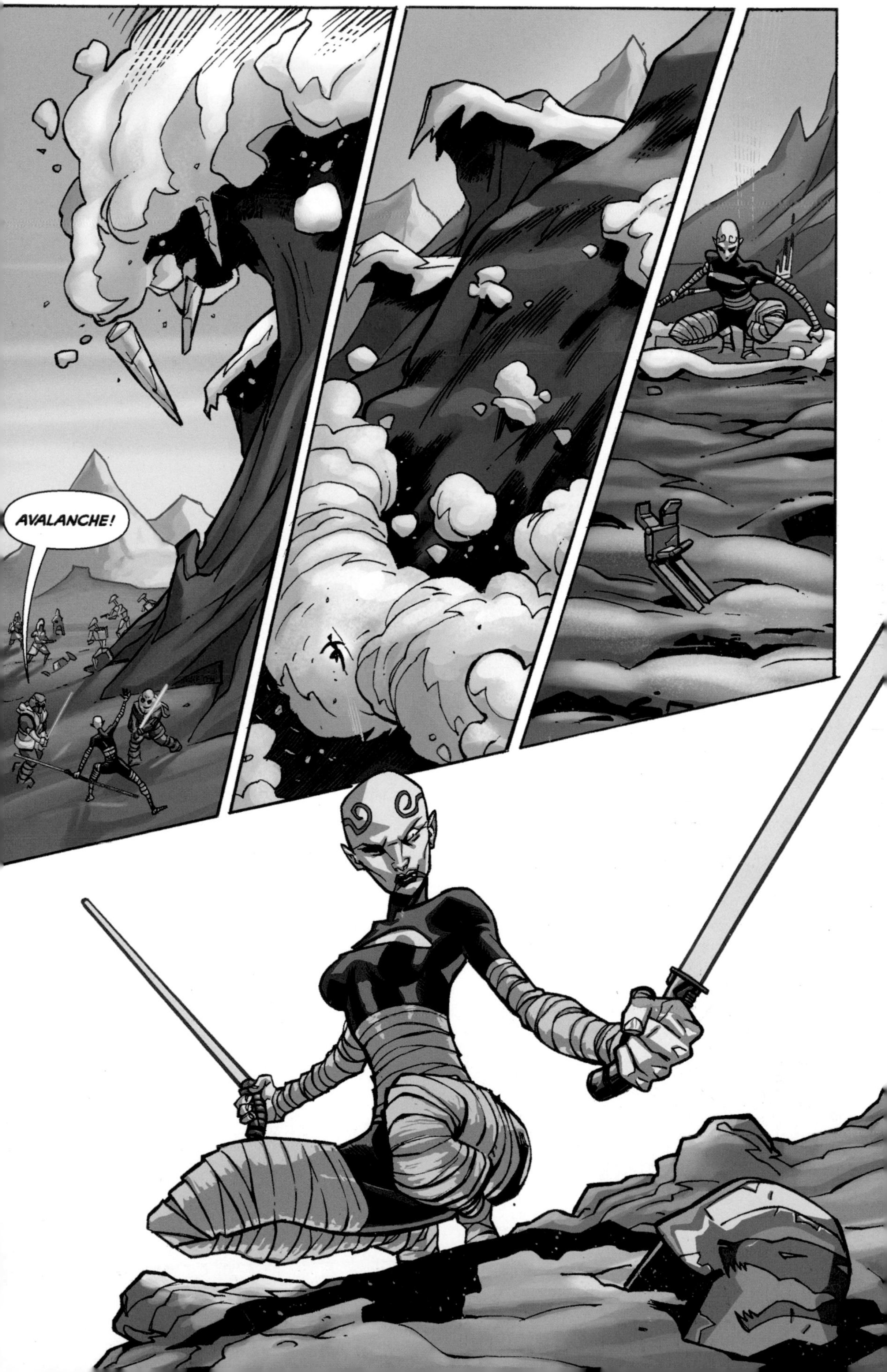
AVALANCHE!

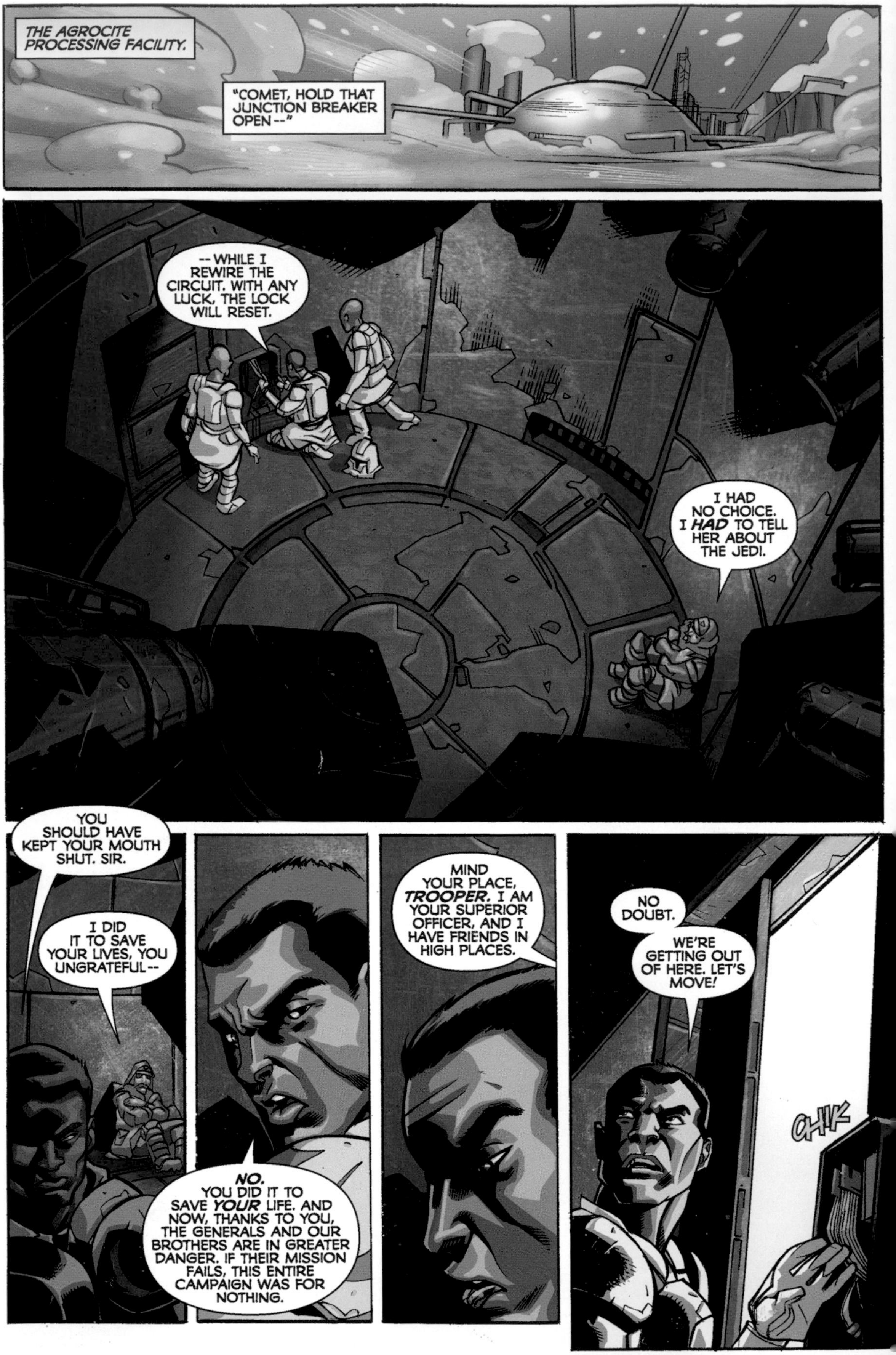
THE AGROCITE PROCESSING FACILITY.
"COMET, HOLD THAT JUNCTION BREAKER OPEN--"
--WHILE I REWIRE THE CIRCUIT. WITH ANY LUCK, THE LOCK WILL RESET.
I HAD NO CHOICE. I HAD TO TELL HER ABOUT THE JEDI.
YOU SHOULD HAVE KEPT YOUR MOUTH SHUT. SIR.
I DID IT TO SAVE YOUR LIVES, YOU UNGRATEFUL--
NO. YOU DID IT TO SAVE YOUR LIFE. AND NOW, THANKS TO YOU, THE GENERALS AND OUR BROTHERS ARE IN GREATER DANGER. IF THEIR MISSION FAILS, THIS ENTIRE CAMPAIGN WAS FOR NOTHING.
MIND YOUR PLACE, TROOPER. I AM YOUR SUPERIOR OFFICER, AND I HAVE FRIENDS IN HIGH PLACES.
NO DOUBT.
WE'RE GETTING OUT OF HERE. LET'S MOVE!
CHIK

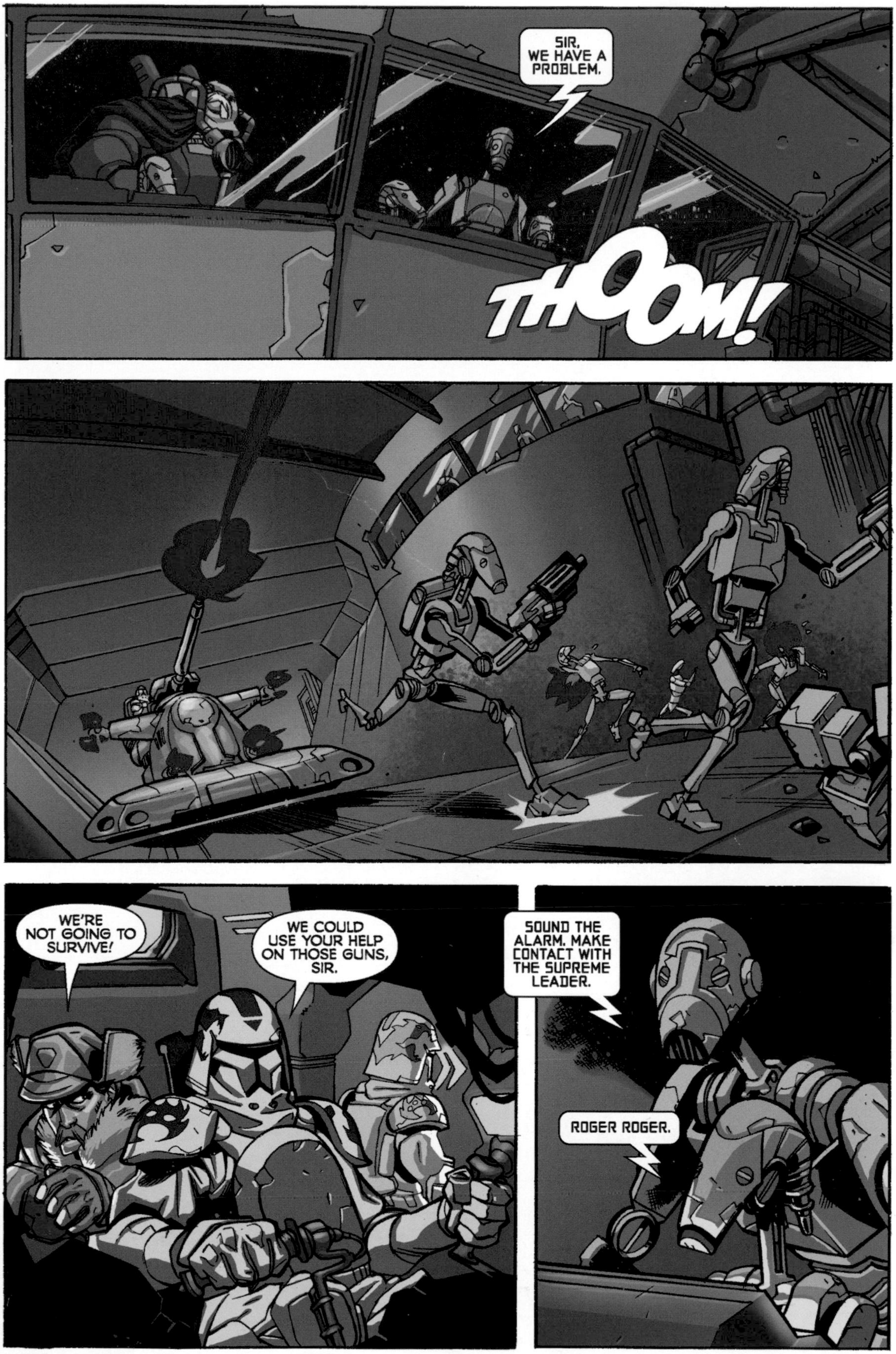
SIR, WE HAVE A PROBLEM.
THOOM!
WE'RE NOT GOING TO SURVIVE!
WE COULD USE YOUR HELP ON THOSE GUNS, SIR.
SOUND THE ALARM. MAKE CONTACT WITH THE SUPREME LEADER.
ROGER ROGER.

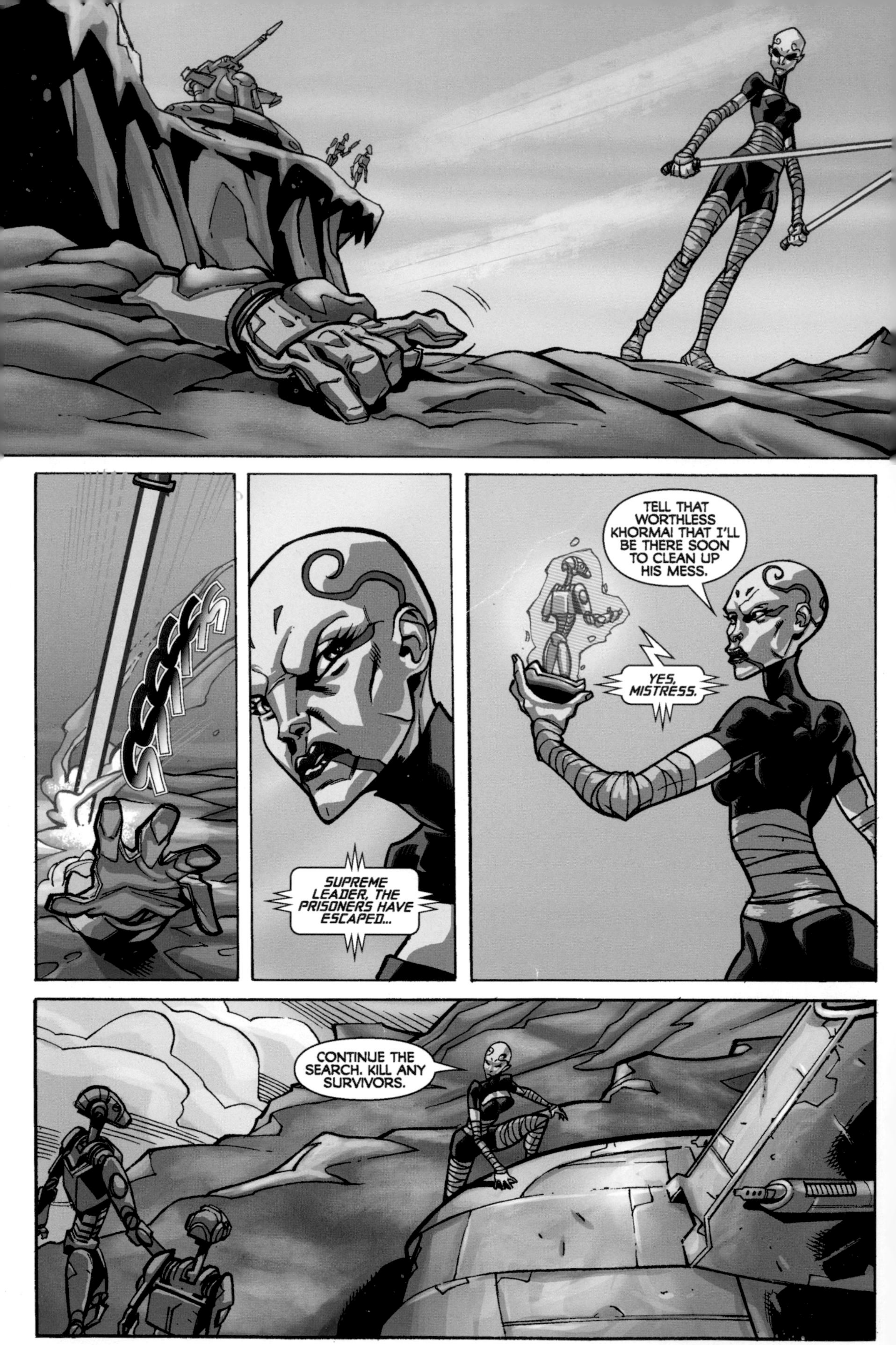
SSSSSS
SUPREME LEADER, THE PRISONERS HAVE ESCAPED...
TELL THAT WORTHLESS KHORMAI THAT I'LL BE THERE SOON TO CLEAN UP HIS MESS.
YES, MISTRESS.
CONTINUE THE SEARCH. KILL ANY SURVIVORS.

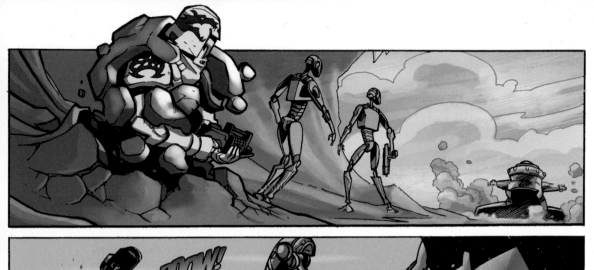

I DON'T KNOW HOW WE SURVIVED THAT ONE.

WE USED THE FORCE TO CREATE A POCKET THAT OFFERED SOME PROTECTION.

HOW IS YOUR ARM, MASTER PLO?

BROKEN. BONES BRITTLE WITH THE PASSING OF AGES.

WE LOST STEN, DEADEYE, BLUNT, AND JARK, AND WORSE -- THE EXPLOSIVES ARE GONE.

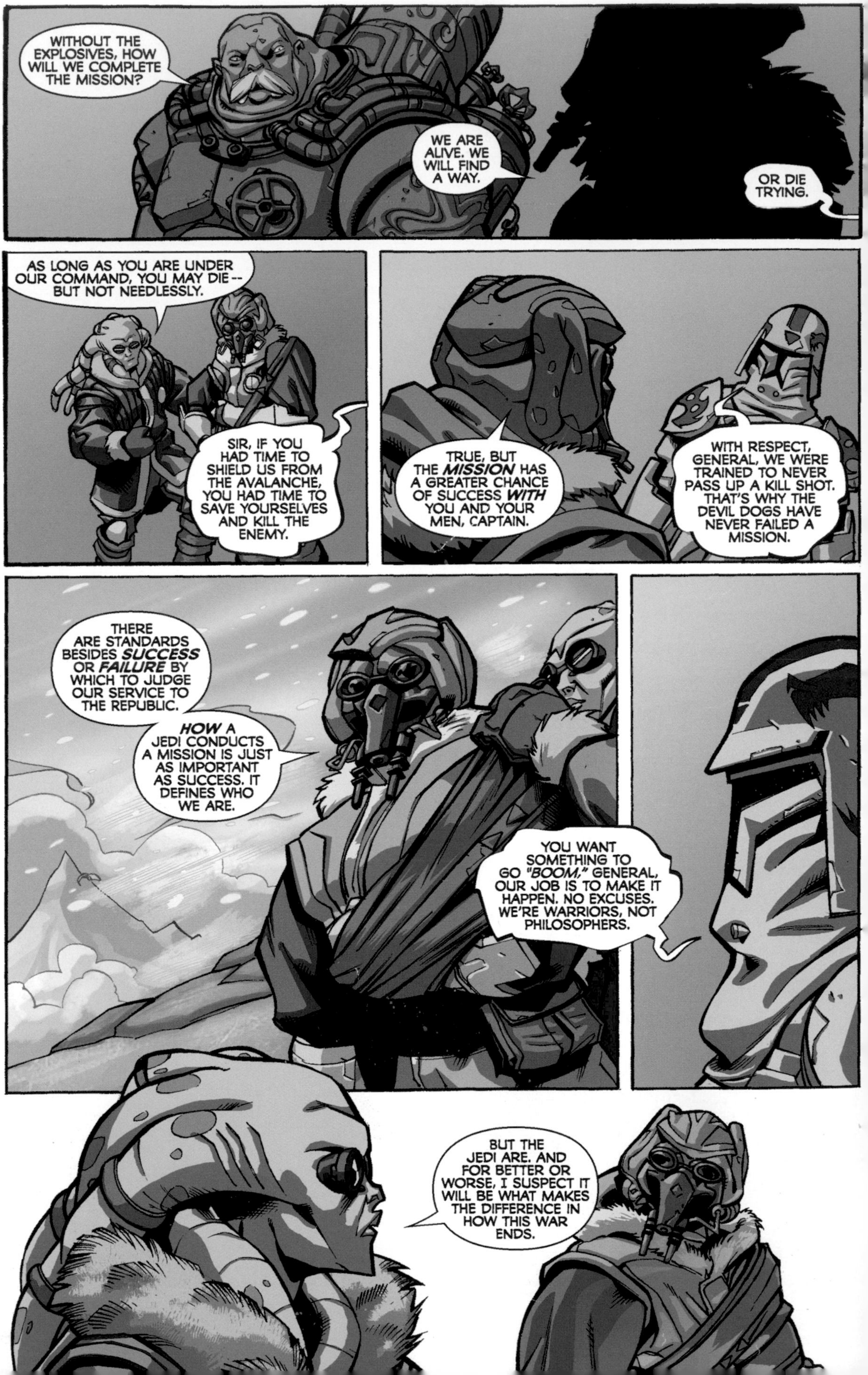
WITHOUT THE EXPLOSIVES, HOW WILL WE COMPLETE THE MISSION?
WE ARE ALIVE. WE WILL FIND A WAY.
OR DIE TRYING.
AS LONG AS YOU ARE UNDER OUR COMMAND, YOU MAY DIE-- BUT NOT NEEDLESSLY.
SIR, IF YOU HAD TIME TO SHIELD US FROM THE AVALANCHE, YOU HAD TIME TO SAVE YOURSELVES AND KILL THE ENEMY.
TRUE, BUT THE *MISSION* HAS A GREATER CHANCE OF SUCCESS *WITH* YOU AND YOUR MEN, CAPTAIN.
WITH RESPECT, GENERAL, WE WERE TRAINED TO NEVER PASS UP A KILL SHOT. THAT'S WHY THE DEVIL DOGS HAVE NEVER FAILED A MISSION.
THERE ARE STANDARDS BESIDES *SUCCESS* OR *FAILURE* BY WHICH TO JUDGE OUR SERVICE TO THE REPUBLIC.
HOW A JEDI CONDUCTS A MISSION IS JUST AS IMPORTANT AS SUCCESS. IT DEFINES WHO WE ARE.
YOU WANT SOMETHING TO GO *"BOOM,"* GENERAL, OUR JOB IS TO MAKE IT HAPPEN. NO EXCUSES. WE'RE WARRIORS, NOT PHILOSOPHERS.
BUT THE JEDI ARE. AND FOR BETTER OR WORSE, I SUSPECT IT WILL BE WHAT MAKES THE DIFFERENCE IN HOW THIS WAR ENDS.

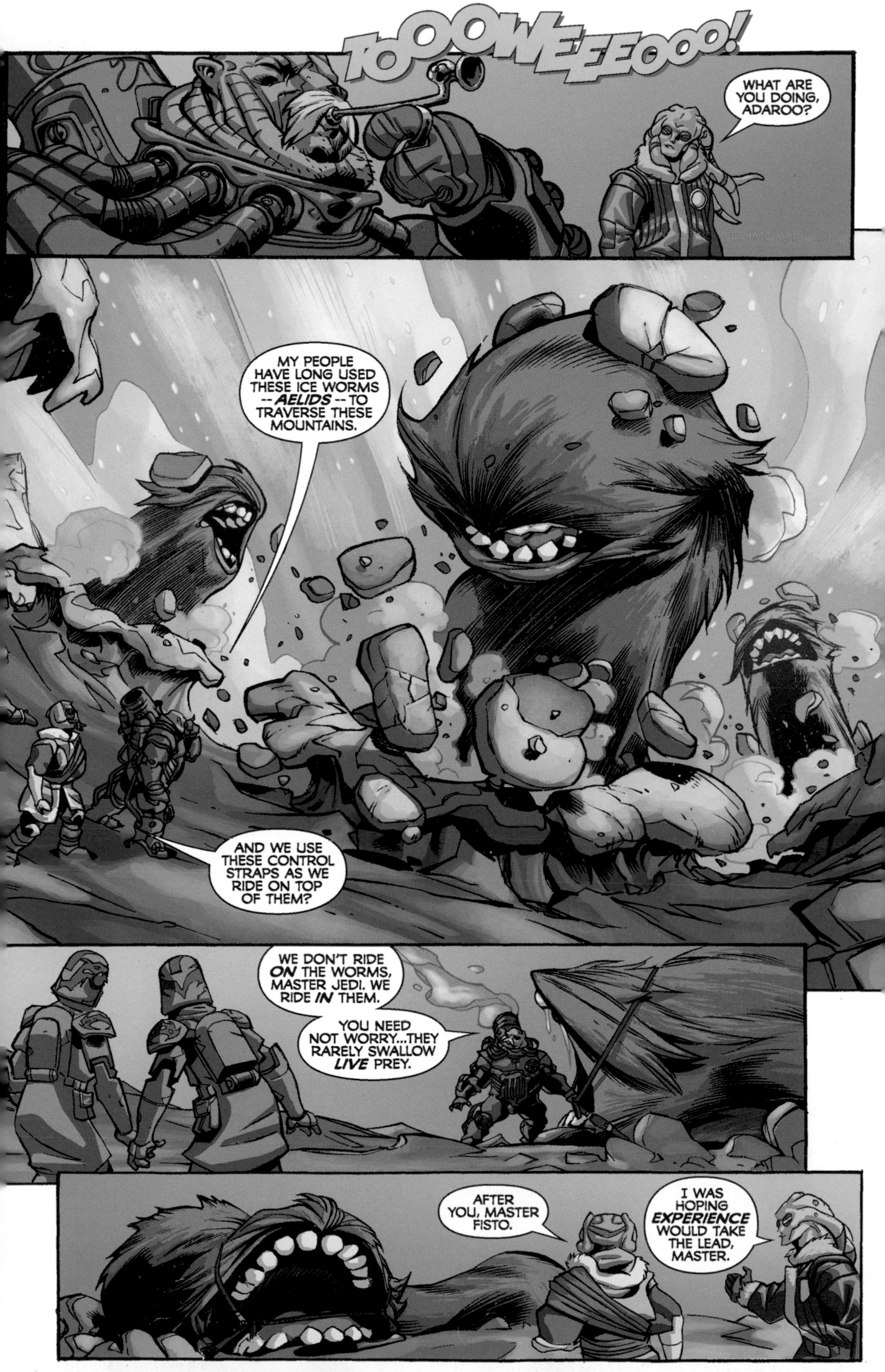
TOOOWEEEOOO!
WHAT ARE YOU DOING, ADAROO?
MY PEOPLE HAVE LONG USED THESE ICE WORMS --AELIDS-- TO TRAVERSE THESE MOUNTAINS.
AND WE USE THESE CONTROL STRAPS AS WE RIDE ON TOP OF THEM?
WE DON'T RIDE ON THE WORMS, MASTER JEDI. WE RIDE IN THEM.
YOU NEED NOT WORRY...THEY RARELY SWALLOW LIVE PREY.
AFTER YOU, MASTER FISTO.
I WAS HOPING EXPERIENCE WOULD TAKE THE LEAD, MASTER.

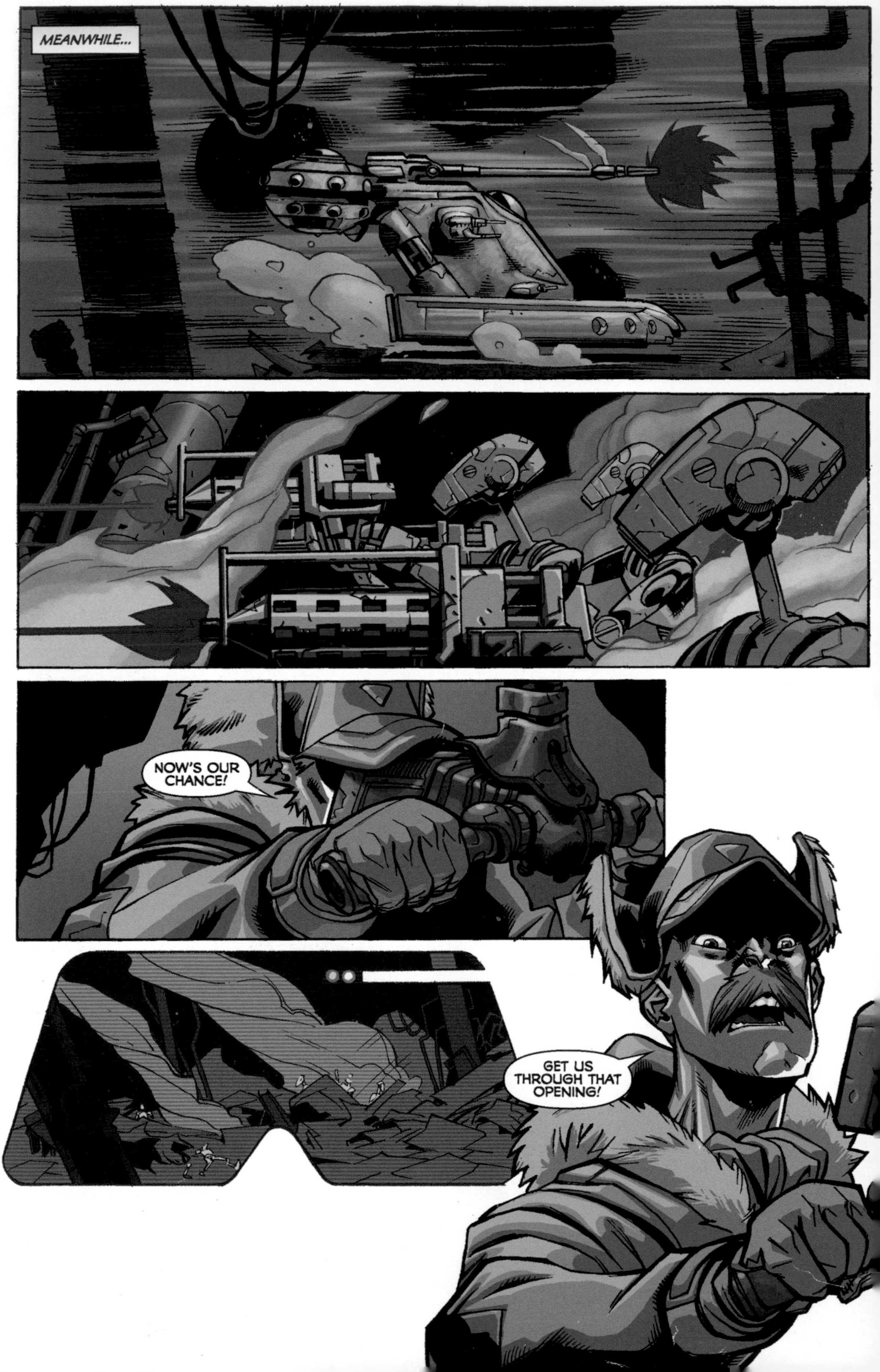
MEANWHILE...
NOW'S OUR CHANCE!
GET US THROUGH THAT OPENING!

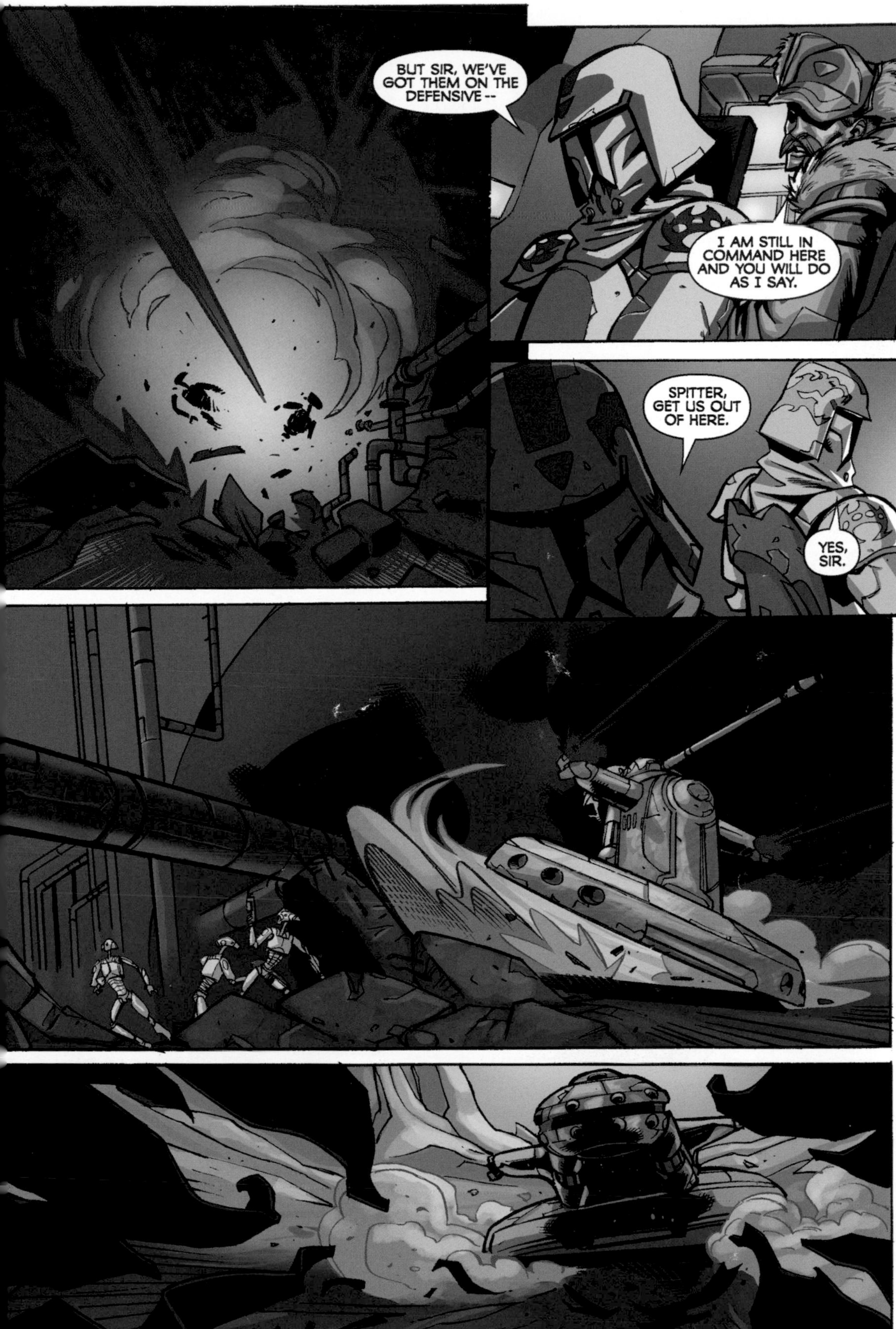
BUT SIR, WE'VE GOT THEM ON THE DEFENSIVE --
I AM STILL IN COMMAND HERE AND YOU WILL DO AS I SAY.
SPITTER, GET US OUT OF HERE.
YES, SIR.

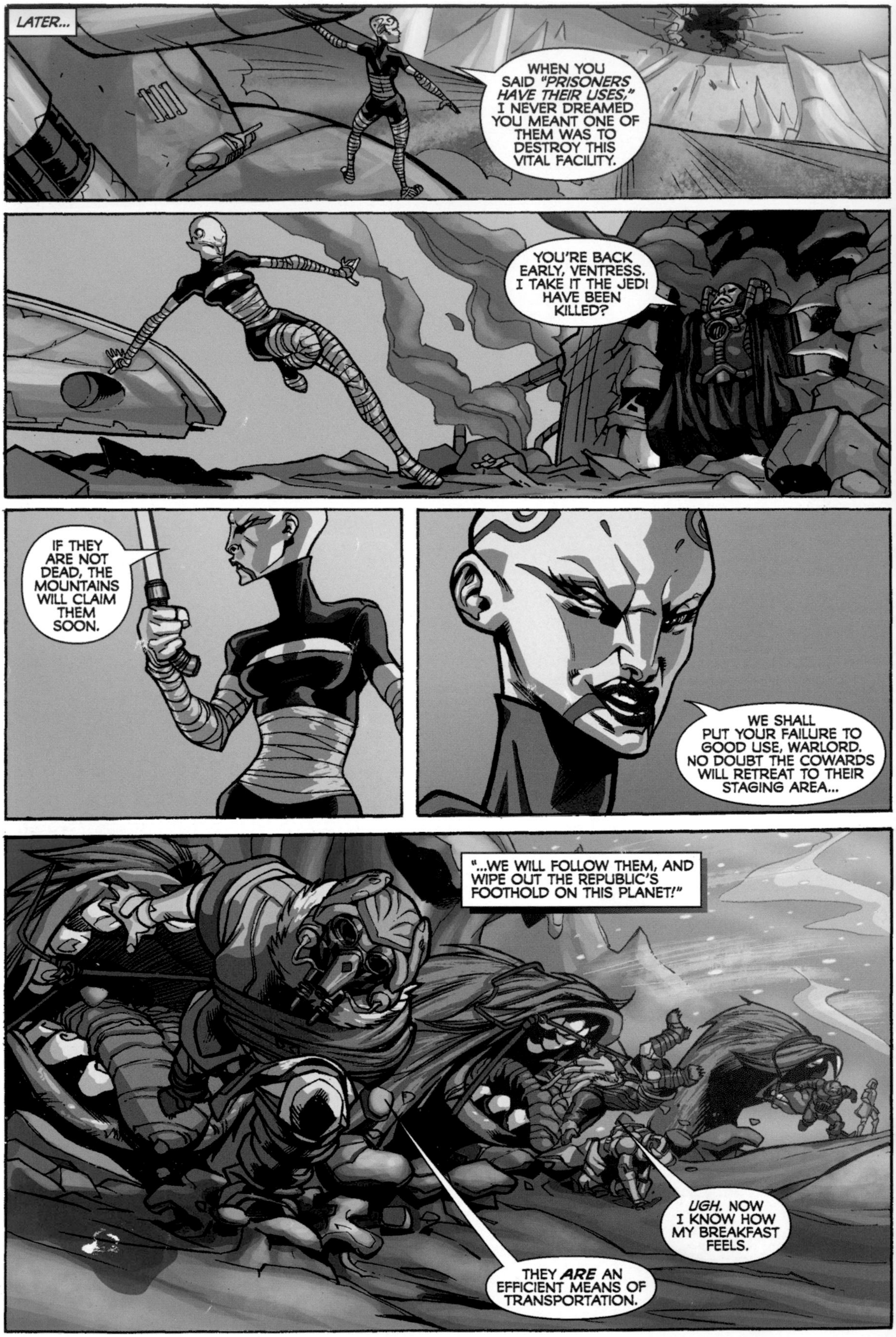
LATER...
WHEN YOU SAID "PRISONERS HAVE THEIR USES," I NEVER DREAMED YOU MEANT ONE OF THEM WAS TO DESTROY THIS VITAL FACILITY.
YOU'RE BACK EARLY, VENTRESS. I TAKE IT THE JEDI HAVE BEEN KILLED?
IF THEY ARE NOT DEAD, THE MOUNTAINS WILL CLAIM THEM SOON.
WE SHALL PUT YOUR FAILURE TO GOOD USE, WARLORD. NO DOUBT THE COWARDS WILL RETREAT TO THEIR STAGING AREA...
"...WE WILL FOLLOW THEM, AND WIPE OUT THE REPUBLIC'S FOOTHOLD ON THIS PLANET!"
UGH. NOW I KNOW HOW MY BREAKFAST FEELS.
THEY ARE AN EFFICIENT MEANS OF TRANSPORTATION.

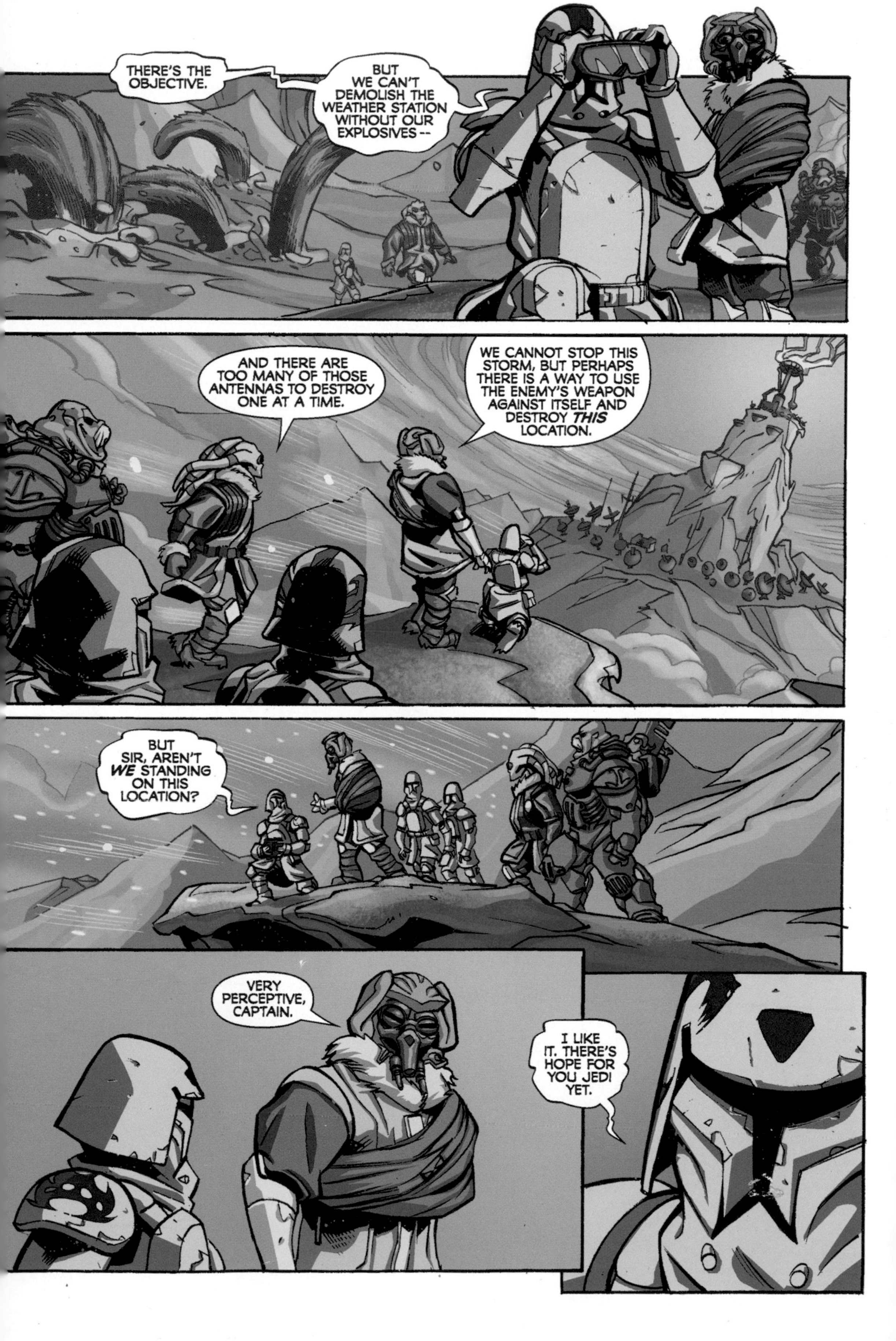
THERE'S THE OBJECTIVE.
BUT WE CAN'T DEMOLISH THE WEATHER STATION WITHOUT OUR EXPLOSIVES --
AND THERE ARE TOO MANY OF THOSE ANTENNAS TO DESTROY ONE AT A TIME.
WE CANNOT STOP THIS STORM, BUT PERHAPS THERE IS A WAY TO USE THE ENEMY'S WEAPON AGAINST ITSELF AND DESTROY *THIS* LOCATION.
BUT SIR, AREN'T *WE* STANDING ON THIS LOCATION?
VERY PERCEPTIVE, CAPTAIN.
I LIKE IT. THERE'S HOPE FOR YOU JEDI YET.

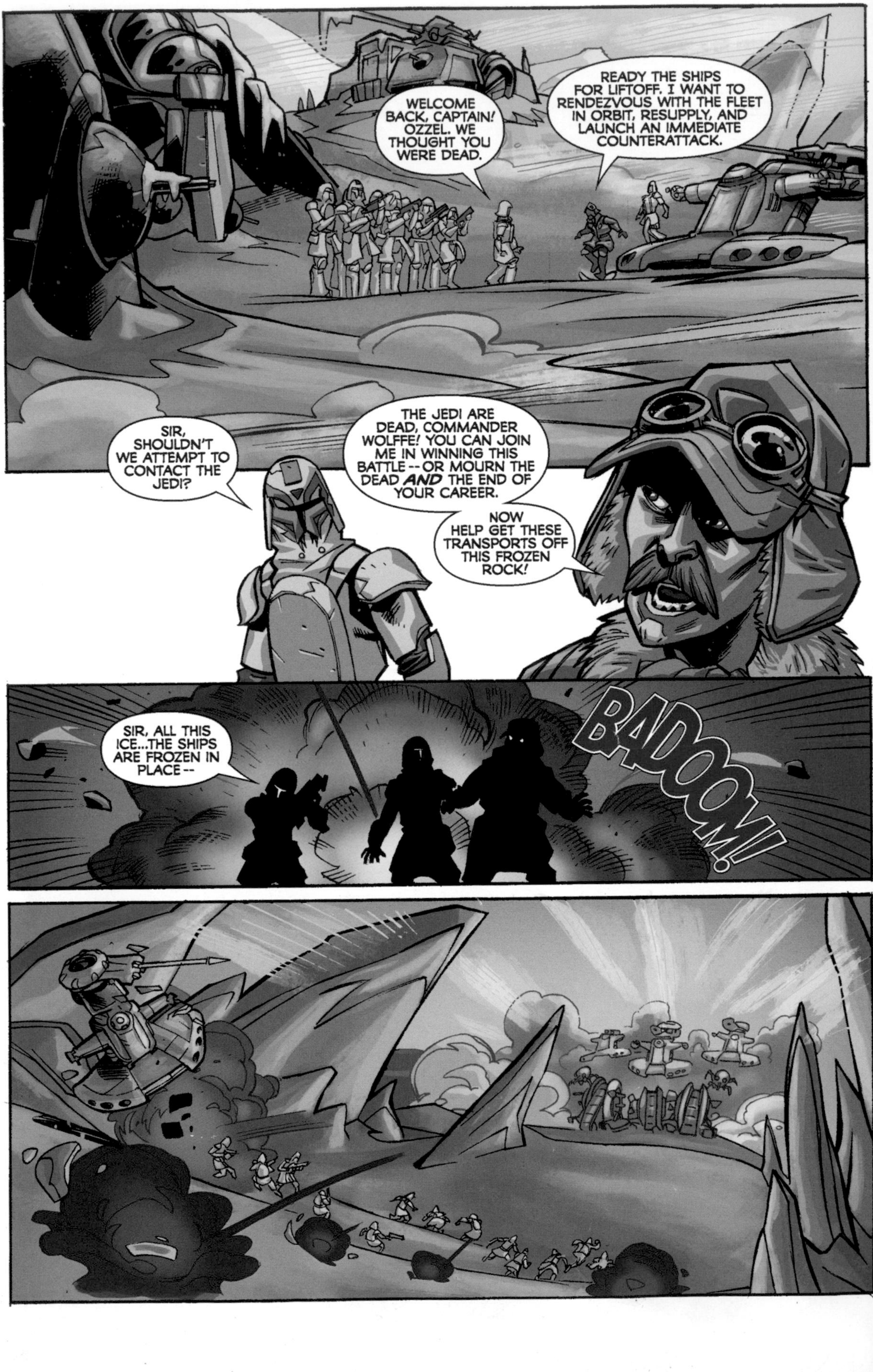
WELCOME BACK, CAPTAIN! OZZEL. WE THOUGHT YOU WERE DEAD.
READY THE SHIPS FOR LIFTOFF. I WANT TO RENDEZVOUS WITH THE FLEET IN ORBIT, RESUPPLY, AND LAUNCH AN IMMEDIATE COUNTERATTACK.
SIR, SHOULDN'T WE ATTEMPT TO CONTACT THE JEDI?
THE JEDI ARE DEAD, COMMANDER WOLFFE! YOU CAN JOIN ME IN WINNING THIS BATTLE -- OR MOURN THE DEAD **AND** THE END OF YOUR CAREER.
NOW HELP GET THESE TRANSPORTS OFF THIS FROZEN ROCK!
SIR, ALL THIS ICE...THE SHIPS ARE FROZEN IN PLACE --
BADOOM!!

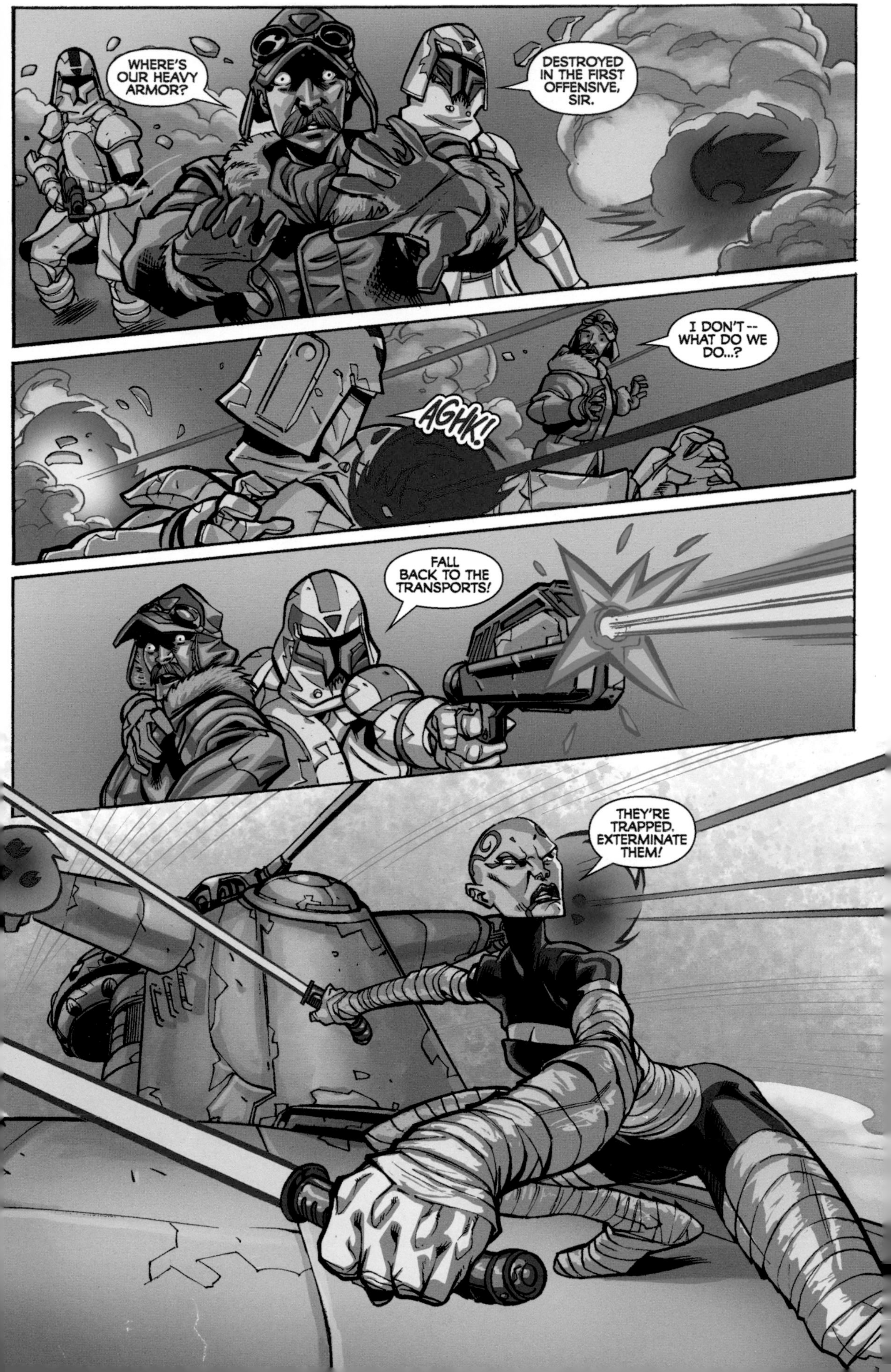
WHERE'S OUR HEAVY ARMOR?
DESTROYED IN THE FIRST OFFENSIVE, SIR.
I DON'T -- WHAT DO WE DO...?
AGHK!
FALL BACK TO THE TRANSPORTS!
THEY'RE TRAPPED. EXTERMINATE THEM!

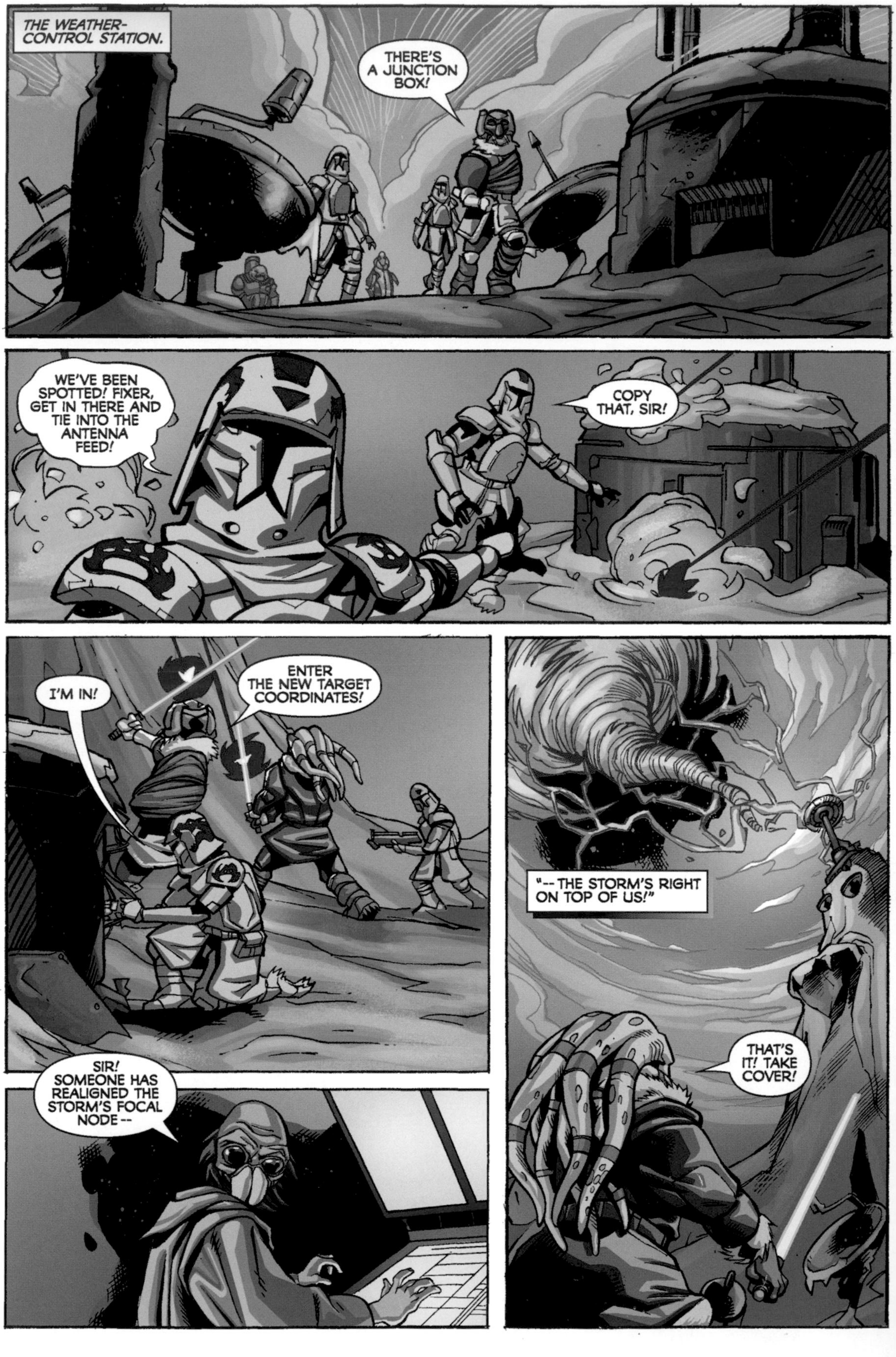
THE WEATHER-CONTROL STATION.
THERE'S A JUNCTION BOX!
WE'VE BEEN SPOTTED! FIXER, GET IN THERE AND TIE INTO THE ANTENNA FEED!
COPY THAT, SIR!
I'M IN!
ENTER THE NEW TARGET COORDINATES!
SIR! SOMEONE HAS REALIGNED THE STORM'S FOCAL NODE --
"-- THE STORM'S RIGHT ON TOP OF US!"
THAT'S IT! TAKE COVER!

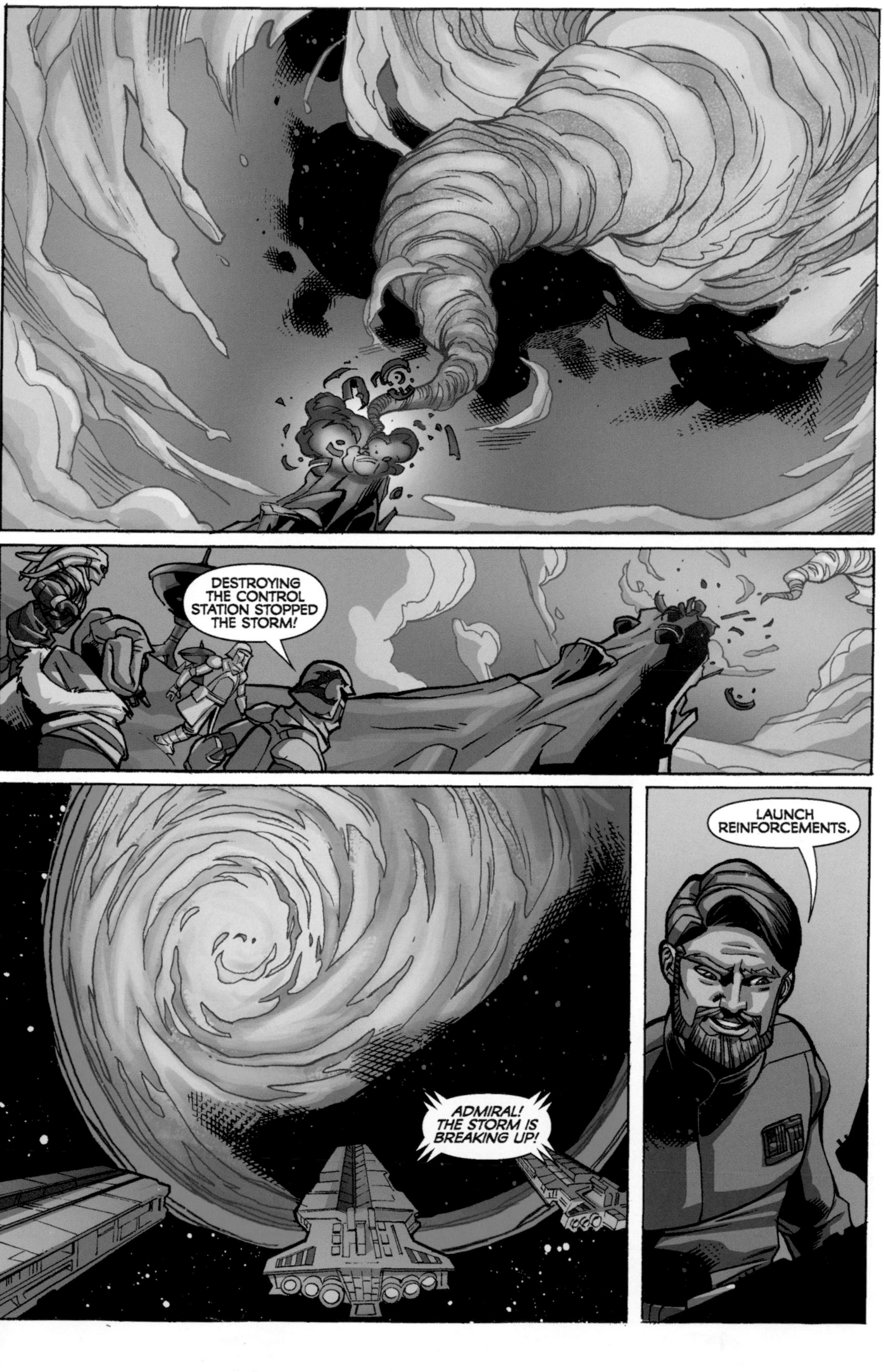
DESTROYING THE CONTROL STATION STOPPED THE STORM!
ADMIRAL! THE STORM IS BREAKING UP!
LAUNCH REINFORCEMENTS.

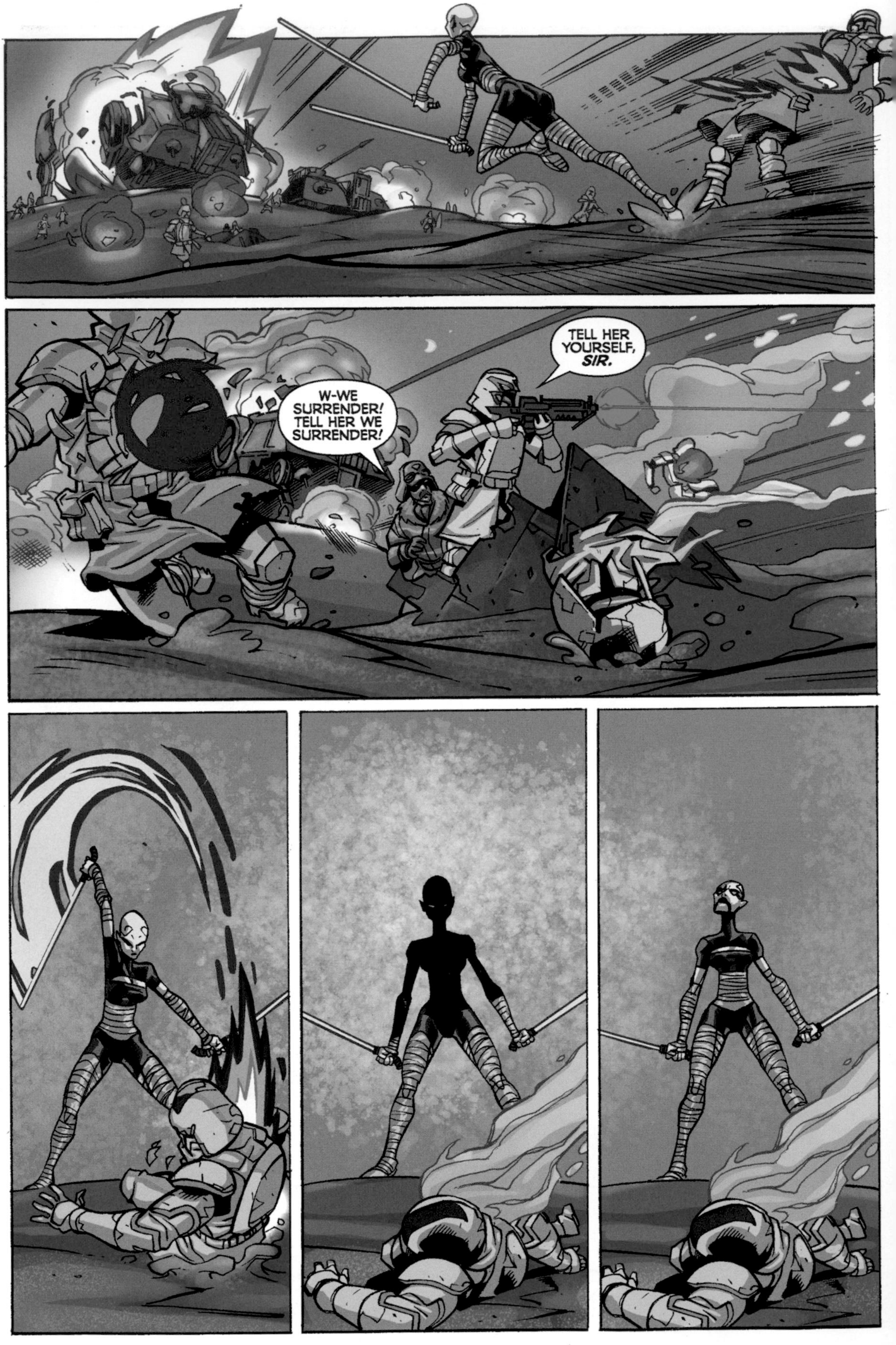
W-WE SURRENDER! TELL HER WE SURRENDER!
TELL HER YOURSELF, SIR.

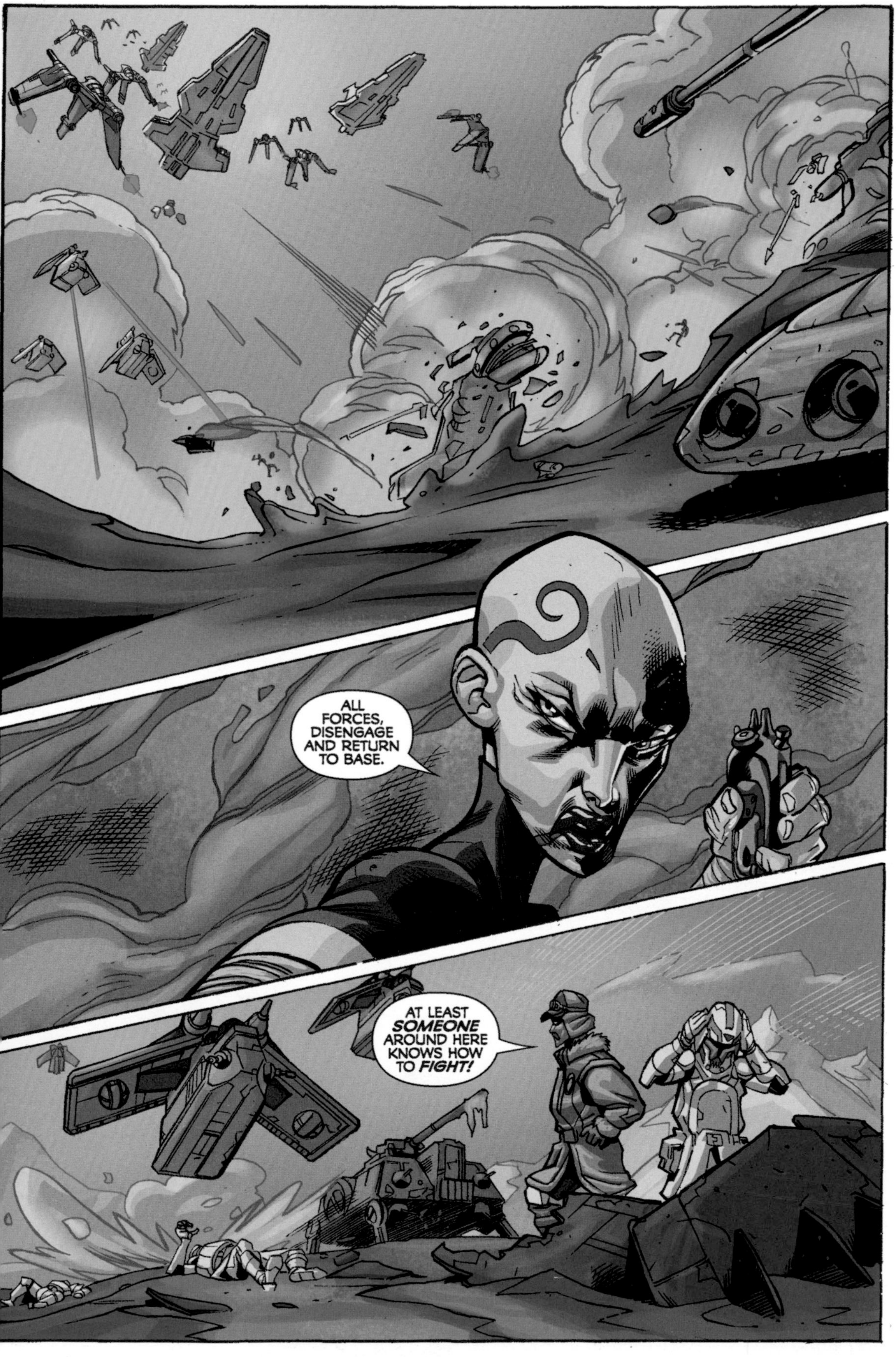
ALL FORCES, DISENGAGE AND RETURN TO BASE.
AT LEAST ***SOMEONE*** AROUND HERE KNOWS HOW TO ***FIGHT!***

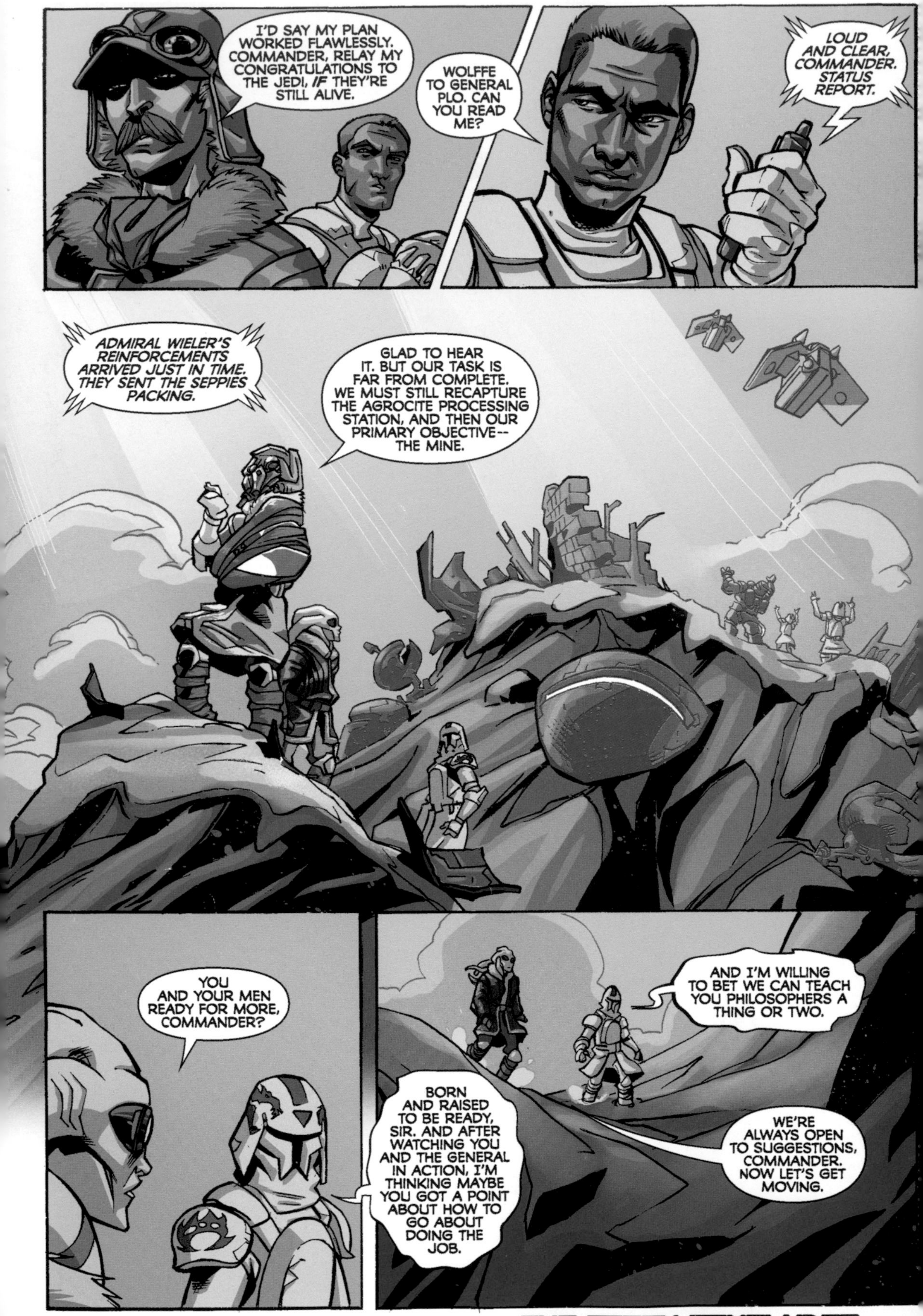
I'D SAY MY PLAN WORKED FLAWLESSLY. COMMANDER, RELAY MY CONGRATULATIONS TO THE JEDI, *IF* THEY'RE STILL ALIVE.
WOLFFE TO GENERAL PLO. CAN YOU READ ME?
LOUD AND CLEAR, COMMANDER. STATUS REPORT.
ADMIRAL WIELER'S REINFORCEMENTS ARRIVED JUST IN TIME. THEY SENT THE SEPPIES PACKING.
GLAD TO HEAR IT. BUT OUR TASK IS FAR FROM COMPLETE. WE MUST STILL RECAPTURE THE AGROCITE PROCESSING STATION, AND THEN OUR PRIMARY OBJECTIVE-- THE MINE.
YOU AND YOUR MEN READY FOR MORE, COMMANDER?
BORN AND RAISED TO BE READY, SIR. AND AFTER WATCHING YOU AND THE GENERAL IN ACTION, I'M THINKING MAYBE YOU GOT A POINT ABOUT HOW TO GO ABOUT DOING THE JOB.
AND I'M WILLING TO BET WE CAN TEACH YOU PHILOSOPHERS A THING OR TWO.
WE'RE ALWAYS OPEN TO SUGGESTIONS, COMMANDER. NOW LET'S GET MOVING.

THE STORY CONCLUDES IN VOLUME 3!